Granny Mae's Christmas Play

Bob Hartman
Illustrated by Lynne Cravath

Granny Mae's

Bob Hartman

◆

Illustrated by
Lynne Cravath

We all put on our costumes. Mine was a little halo made out of Christmas tree tinsel and one of Grampa Joe's huge white dress shirts. "18 neck, 35 long." That's what the label read. And when I put the shirt on, it almost touched the floor. I was the angel Gabriel.

"Everybody into the kitchen!" commanded Granny Mae. "Caitlin, you sit
at the table. Pretend you're chopping carrots or something."

"But I hate carrots!" Caitlin moaned.

Granny Mae ignored her. "And you, Kevin," she continued. "Hide your-
self there in the bottom of the pantry."

I did what Granny Mae told me, but I left the door open—just a crack—
so I could see.

My older cousin Caitlin was Mary. She wore Granny Mae's blue bathrobe and a white towel on her head. The towel was held fast with one of those bungee cords that Grampa Joe always uses to keep his trunk shut.

"Many years ago," Granny Mae began, "there lived a girl named Mary. She was a good girl." And Caitlin snickered, because *she* actually wasn't very good at all!

"One day, an angel named Gabriel stopped by to visit her." Granny snapped her fingers, and I leaped out of the pantry.

I started to go back into the pantry, but Granny Mae shook her head. "No, Kevin. Upstairs, to the big bedroom." Then she pointed at my older brother, Brian. "You, too. And hurry! Kevin in the closet, and Brian on the bed."

Brian wore Grampa Joe's bathrobe, with one of Grampa's old hammers hanging from the belt, and, in his hurry, he tripped halfway up the steps.

When everyone else had squeezed into the bedroom, Granny Mae started the story again. "Now, Mary was supposed to get married to a carpenter named Joseph."

"Yecchh!" whispered Brian. "She's my cousin!"

But Granny hushed him and went on. "When Joseph found out that Mary was going to have a baby, he figured she'd been seeing another man. So he decided to call the wedding off. That is, until he had a midnight visit from our friend Gabriel."

"Nine months passed," Granny continued. And my Aunt Robin walked by with a big cardboard "9" around her neck and a calendar in her hands. "And just as Mary was about to have her baby [Caitlin jammed a pillow under her robe], Joseph came home from work with some bad news."

Brian cleared his throat and said as sadly as he could, "We have to go to Bethlehem, Mary. Sixty miles away!"

"Why?" asked Granny Mae. "Because the Roman Emperor wanted to count everybody in his kingdom. And to make it easier, everyone had to go back to his or her hometown—which, in Joseph's case, meant Bethlehem. Mary had to go with him because she was his wife. So Joseph saddled up his donkey."

"Finally," said Granny Mae, "they came to a place where the innkeeper was a little more friendly. Instead of telling them to get lost, he showed them the way to his stable."

And, with that, Uncle Evan opened the door to the garage. We walked in, and there, in front of Grampa Joe's restored '65 Mustang, sat a little doll's crib filled with hay.

"Places, everyone!" ordered Granny Mae.

And so we sang—not just the angels, but all of us—"Hark the Herald
Angels Sing" and "Joy to the World." Drivers flashed their car lights as they
went by. And some of the neighbors even stuck their heads out their doors
and watched.

"When the angels went away," said Granny, "the shepherds went to
Bethlehem to find the baby in the manger."

So we jumped off the ladder (just missing the pink flamingo!) and
everybody went back into the garage.

Notes for Readers

Your family can join in Granny Mae's Christmas play, too. Or your neighbors. Or your Sunday school. Or your youth group.

You'll need plenty of paper bags, for a start—or wrapping paper, if you would like to give each actor a "present." Put the name of the role (Joseph, Gabriel . . .) on a piece of paper. Write out the actor's lines as well. Put the role, lines, costume, and props in each bag. I have tried to keep the costumes simple—limited to things that can be found around most homes. But feel free to make them more elaborate, and use

your imagination to come up with different ways to make horns or halos or little lamb's hoofs. You might also want to include the words to the carols you intend to sing.

Choose your actors carefully. For instance, you'll need someone with a strong back and a good sense of humor to play the donkey. But, once again, have fun with this part of the play, and don't be afraid to cast against type. A couple of big burly guys might make great angels—or little lambs, for that matter!

Like Granny Mae, the narrator is really the director, too, and should be thoroughly familiar with the story. There's no need for that person to memorize lines—she or he will have enough to do just running the show. It would be helpful, however, if that person were good at improvising and taking advantage of the

"moments" that will surely arise.
As far as the settings go, you will need to adapt
the script to your own situation. If your house
doesn't lead directly to the garage, then
you may need to find another room for
the stable or go outside sooner. Once
again, use your imagination, and if
you want to decorate each room
to make it look more like a "set,"
that's fine—though I do think
there is something simple and
wonderful and true about setting
the story of God's arrival among
us in places that are ordinary,
common, and familiar.

You might also want to consider
making this event a surprise—
just like Granny Mae did.
Some participants may not
appreciate this, so you may
need to warn them. But some
groups will enjoy the surprise
and, perhaps, participate more
willingly because they have not had to
worry about it ahead of time. Don't force
anyone to join in, of course, but a little gentle
coaxing goes a long way.

Above all, have fun with this little play, and pray that it not only brings your
group closer together, but that it brings them closer to the meaning of
Christmas as well.